For my darling Jack

Written and illustrated by Rebecca Donaldson

Published by RD Publishing, Melbourne, Australia

When you were little
the world was quite strange;

the hustle and bustling
stopped, for a change.

Everything paused
and we all stayed inside;

something was scary –
we all had to hide.

When you were little
we all covered our faces;

we couldn't see friends
and we couldn't go places.

We all stayed apart
and stayed home every day,

and got used to life
in this funny new way.

When you were little
it was always just us;

we'd play and we'd cuddle
and sing when you'd fuss.

We stayed in our home,
learnt about one another,

And when things got lonely,
we had each other.

Now the world's better
(and it took quite a while)

I remember that time
and it makes me smile

to know that in hard times –
and this part is true...

I got through it all
because I love you.